This edition published by Parragon Books Ltd in 2013
Parragon
Chartist House
15-17 Trim Street
Bath BA1 1HA, UK
www.parragon.com

Edited by Sarah Mellowes
Designed by Jonathan Ladd
Production by Emma Fulleylove

ISBN 978-1-4454-8622-2

Printed in China

Storybook Collection

PaRragon

Bath · New York · Singapore · Hong Kong · Cologne · Delhi
Melbourne · Amsterdam · Johannesburg · Shenzhen

Contents

The Team Unites

The Samurai Power Rangers were busy training at the Shiba House. As Mike watched Jayden and Kevin practising together, he felt as if he would never be able to use his senses as well as they could. Feeling sad, Mike crept off to see his old buddies down at the amusement arcade.

Meanwhile, deep in the Netherworld, in his ship on the Sanzu River, Master Xandred was busy putting Nighlok to work. Having only recently reawakened, he was not yet strong enough to travel into the human world himself, so instead he sent Nighlok monsters to unleash misery on the world.

   "Let the tears of those crybaby humans fill the Sanzu River until it floods the world," he bellowed.

   To help make this happen, he sent the giant-fisted Rofer through a gap into our world.

Back in our world, Mike was sitting with his old friends trying to make them see how he felt. But when he tried to explain about protecting the world from evil, his friends thought he was talking about a video game.

Suddenly, there was a loud smash nearby and a giant fist came flying up through the pavement, followed by its owner, Rofer. Everybody ran away screaming, all except for Mike, who leaped into action right away.

"I'll take care of this Nighlok on my own," he thought as he ran towards Rofer, pulling his Samuraizer from his pocket.

"Samuraizer! Go, Go Samurai!" he shouted as he ran along, using the magic tool to write the Forest Kanji Symbol that would morph him into the Green Samurai Ranger.

Mike did his best to fight Rofer, but the Nighlok's long arms could travel underground and come up for surprise attacks!

"I'm as cool as an iceberg, but I sting like a bee. It's tough to stop what you can't see!" gloated Rofer as his fist came smashing out of the ground, sending the Green Ranger flying through the air.

"If only I could use my senses as well as Jayden can," thought Mike. "There's no way I can defeat this Nighlok on my own."

Back at the Shiba House, the Samurai Rangers were alerted to Rofer's presence by the Gap Sensor and pinpointed the Nighlok's location on a special locator map. The rest of the team arrived to help the Green Ranger, but just as they did, the Nighlok began to dehydrate. When a Nighlok is away from the Sanzu River for too long, it starts to dry up.

"Uh-oh! Feels like I'm starting to dry out," said Rofer. "Guess I'd better punch out for now. Later, Rangers!"

And with that, he squirmed his way back into the Netherworld.

Back at the Shiba House again, Jayden spoke to Mike.

"You must stay away from your friends and family," Jayden explained. "It's the only way to protect them from evil."

Mike realized this was true and felt sad, but there was work to be done. He knew he had to find a way of sensing a Nighlok's attack before it comes, and he went away on his own to practise.

Meanwhile, back in the Netherworld, Rofer was bathing in the Sanzu River to recharge his power.

"Now I'm gonna pound those Samurai Rangers into chopped liver!" said Rofer. "With the misery I'm gonna cause, soon this river will be fit to burst with human tears!"

When Rofer and the Moogers entered our world again, the Gap Sensor lit up. It didn't take long for the team to morph into the Samurai Rangers, but Mike still wanted to defeat Rofer by himself.

"We've got to help him," said the Pink Ranger.

Grabbing their Spin Swords, the Samurai Rangers used their special powers against the Moogers, quickly defeating them, and leaving Rofer battling the Green Ranger.

"Bring it on, long arms," the Green Ranger yelled at his opponent. Rofer didn't wait to be asked twice, and one of his fists was soon smashing its way underground towards the Green Ranger. Rofer was surprised when the Green Ranger started running away from him. The Green Ranger ran around and around, and Rofer's arm chased him wherever he went. Pretty soon, Rofer's arm was a tangled mess! But the Green Ranger had forgotten Rofer's other arm, which nearly caught him.

Just in time, the Red Ranger arrived, stopping the second arm.

"Time to give you a taste of my Spin Sword," said the Green Ranger as he grabbed his weapon. "Spin Sword – Forest Vortex!" he yelled, using his special attack on the Nighlok. With Rofer's arms still in a tangle, the Green Ranger soon defeated him.

The other Samurai Rangers congratulated the Green Ranger, but the battle wasn't over yet.

"Time for round two," said the Red Ranger. "He's coming back as a MegaMonster!"

The Green Ranger was still determined to defeat Rofer by himself. He grabbed his Samuraizer and FoldingZord so that he could go into MegaMode.

"Bear FoldingZord – MegaMode Power!" he shouted as he wrote the Kanji Symbol that means 'large' over the Zord and morphed into MegaMode.

With the Green Ranger at the helm of the BearZord, he battled Rofer while the others watched.

"We can't let him do this alone," said the Blue Ranger, and the other Samurai Rangers morphed into MegaMode as well.

"Rangers, we need to combine!" shouted the Red Ranger. "Zords, combine!" he commanded as he wrote the Kanji to combine the five Zords into the awesome Megazord.

"Samurai Megazord, we are united!" the Rangers all called out together.

Now they could fight Rofer as a team.

"Now, let's focus," said the Red Ranger. "If we work together we can use our instincts to sense Rofer's next move."

"What's the matter, did you fall asleep?" taunted Rofer. "Well, here comes your wake-up call!"

But as Rofer threw his mighty fist at the Megazord, the Rangers were ready for him. Anticipating his move, the Samurai Rangers soon had the MegaMonster all wrapped up. By working together they had won.

Back at the Shiba House, Jayden, Mia, Emily and Kevin all told Mike what a good job he'd done defeating Rofer.

"The way you got his arms all tangled up was so great," laughed Mia.

But Mike couldn't take all the credit.

"I only stopped one of his arms," Mike told the other Rangers. "It was Jayden who stopped the other arm. I couldn't have defeated Rofer on my own."

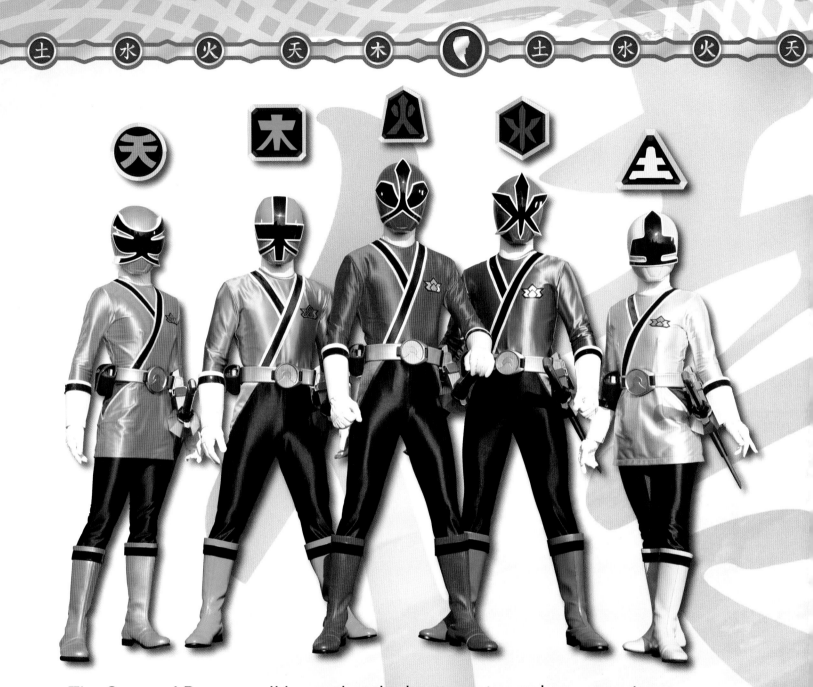

The Samurai Rangers all knew that the best way to work was as a team.
"Rangers together, Samurai forever!" they shouted as one proud voice.

Deal with a Nighlok

One morning at the Shiba House, Emily and Kevin were training together and Mike was working on his Symbol Power. Kevin was in a strange mood.

"If you ever need to talk about missing your old life, you can count on me to be there for you," Kevin told the other Rangers.

Everyone was puzzled; although it was sweet of Kevin to be concerned, this wasn't like him at all.

"He's been acting like this since yesterday," Mentor Ji told the Rangers.

Meanwhile, in the murky depths of the Netherworld, an ugly Nighlok named Doubletone was basking in the waters of the Sanzu River.

"Humans are such crybabies when they're scared," laughed Doubletone as he swam towards Master Xandred's ship.

"What are you doing here, Doubletone?" roared Master Xandred. "I didn't summon you!"

Octoroo explained that he had been the one to summon the ugly Nighlok.

"His face breaks a lot of mirrors, but I hear he's a heartbreaker, too!" he told Master Xandred and Dayu.

Octoroo went on to explain that Doubletone has the power to make human beings give up on their dreams.

"Nothing makes a human sadder than giving up on a dream," said Doubletone. "Soon the Sanzu River will be so full you won't know what to do with it all."

"Get on with it then," commanded Master Xandred. "Failure is NOT an option!"

Back in our world, a little boy sat alone in a park, holding on tight to a baseball key ring that his father had given him. Suddenly, he noticed a glowing light coming out of a nearby tree. It was Doubletone.

"Aargh! A monster!" cried the boy.

"I may be a monster, but I'm just here to make a deal," said Doubletone as he squeezed his way out of the tree trunk.

The young boy listened to the evil Nighlok as he explained what the deal was.

Back at the Shiba House, the Gap Sensor was flashing to let the Rangers know that a monster had entered our world. Mentor Ji opened the locator map, which showed where the monster was. In a matter of moments, the Samurai Rangers were on the scene.

"Run away as fast as you can," Emily told the boy.

"I wasn't going to hurt him," said Doubletone. "We were just making a deal."

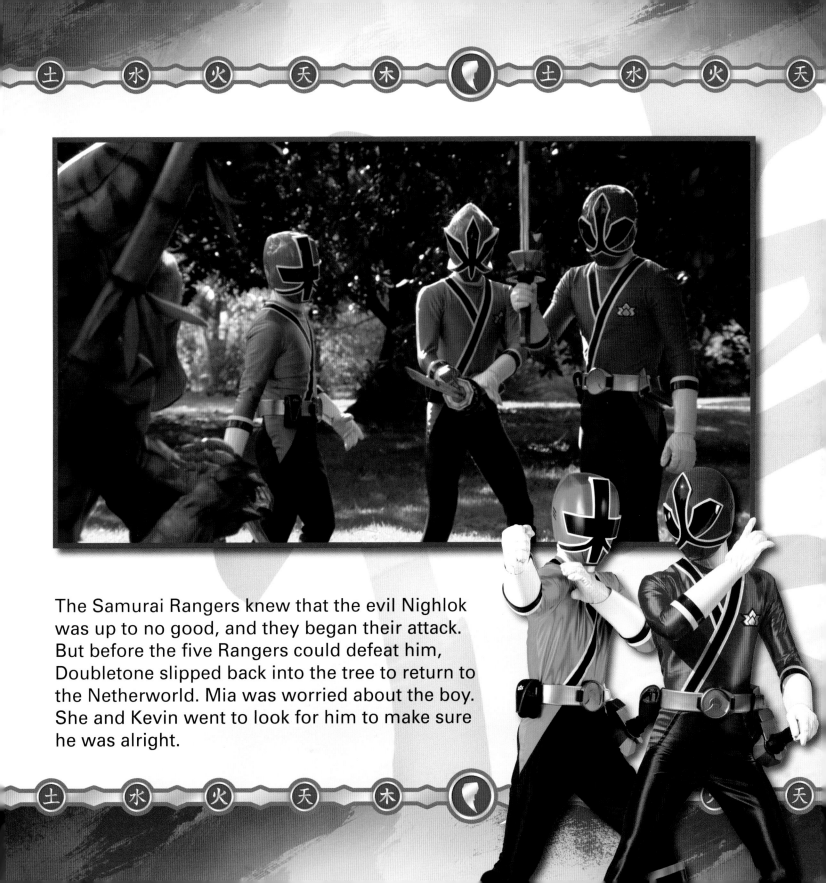

The Samurai Rangers knew that the evil Nighlok was up to no good, and they began their attack. But before the five Rangers could defeat him, Doubletone slipped back into the tree to return to the Netherworld. Mia was worried about the boy. She and Kevin went to look for him to make sure he was alright.

Down in the Netherworld, Doubletone was boasting to Dayu about what he had done.

"This kid I met dreams of playing baseball. Tell Master Xandred I'm gonna grandslam that kid's dreams!"

"So get going and play ball!" yelled Dayu.

天 天 天
天

Meanwhile, Mia and Kevin had found the boy and were trying to find out what deal he had made with Doubletone. The boy wouldn't tell them anything, but the Rangers decided to keep an eye on him. They found out that the boy was getting ready for a big baseball game, and they could see how important the game was to him.

Kevin told Mia that he could understand how the kid felt; in his old life, he had big dreams of becoming an Olympic swimmer.

"It's tough giving up on a dream," he told Mia.

"One day, when we've defeated the Nighlok monsters, we can go back to our old lives and our dreams," said Mia.

She felt sorry for Kevin and suddenly realized the reason he had been behaving strangely – it was because he missed his old life. Knowing the evil Nighlok would soon return, they decided to keep a watch on the boy's house.

When the boy came out of his house the next day, Kevin and Mia were surprised to see him throwing his baseball kit into the rubbish bin.

"Don't you have a game today?" asked Mia kindly.

"No, I've given up playing baseball," replied the boy, who seemed very sad.

The two Rangers tried to find out why he would give up on his dream, but the boy still wouldn't tell them a thing.

Just then, Doubletone appeared, laughing.

"I made him give up on his dream and soon the Sanzu River will be flooded with all the tears he will cry! Ha!" laughed Doubletone.

"But you said if I gave up baseball, my dad would come home," cried the poor boy, who told Mia and Kevin that his dad was in the army and had to go away for a while.

"You can't bring his dad back," yelled Mia angrily. "You lied to this kid!"

Mia told the boy to run away as they prepared to fight the Nighlok.

"Samuraizer – Go, Go Samurai!" Mia and Kevin shouted together as they wrote the magic Kanji Symbols that would morph them into Samurai Rangers.

The two Rangers battled bravely, but Doubletone was a very powerful Nighlok and he sent them flying with his Tiger Tidal Wave. Luckily, the other Rangers arrived in the nick of time to help their friends. Doubletone was outnumbered, but he had another trick up his sleeve.

"Moogers! Come out, come out, wherever you are," he sang playfully, and right away Moogers began springing up from the ground until the Rangers were surrounded.

However, the Moogers were no match for the Rangers' special weapons. The Red Ranger blasted a group of Moogers with his Fire Smasher, and the Green and the Yellow Ranger defeated the rest with their Samurai weapons. Now they had to fight Doubletone, and the Blue and Pink Rangers wasted no time finishing him off.

But the battle wasn't quite over yet. The Samurai Rangers knew only too well that when a Nighlok is defeated, it comes back as a MegaMonster – but they were ready for him! In a few moments, all five Rangers had morphed into MegaMode.

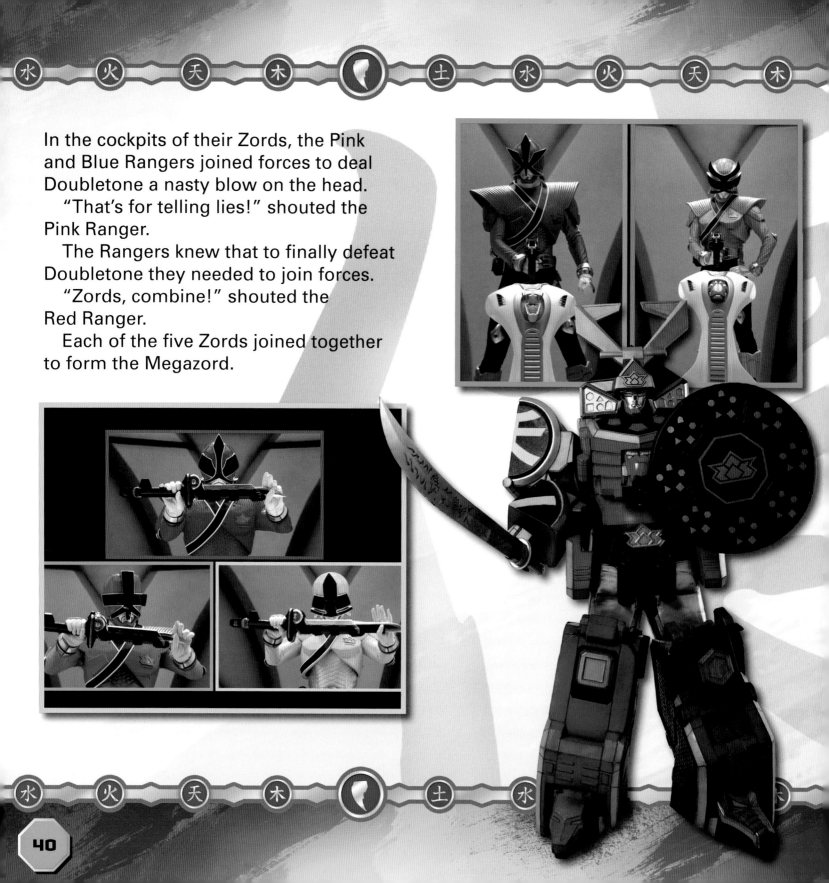

In the cockpits of their Zords, the Pink and Blue Rangers joined forces to deal Doubletone a nasty blow on the head.

"That's for telling lies!" shouted the Pink Ranger.

The Rangers knew that to finally defeat Doubletone they needed to join forces.

"Zords, combine!" shouted the Red Ranger.

Each of the five Zords joined together to form the Megazord.

However, Doubletone was a powerful opponent, and with one mighty blow, he knocked the Megazord's sword out of reach. The Blue Ranger used his DragonZord to do a Dragon Leap high into the air. Next, Mia took the chance to launch an aerial Turtle Strike which landed a massive blow to the MegaMonster's head. Now the Megazord could grab back his mighty sword, and with a few cleverly aimed blows, Doubletone was defeated.

While the Rangers had been fighting Doubletone, the boy had run off to his baseball game. When he got there, he found that the rubbish collectors had handed in his baseball kit. He could play in his game after all! The boy was very happy, especially as all five Rangers were there to watch, even if his dad couldn't be there.

Jayden had one last trick up his sleeve. Taking his Samuraizer, he wrote a special Kanji Symbol in the air and, as if by magic, the boy's father appeared in a glowing light.

"Go get 'em, Tiger," the dad told his son before the image faded.

Beaming with happiness, the boy rushed away to join his team.

"How did you do that?" asked Mike.

"I just helped a dream become a vision," replied Jayden. "You should never give up on your dreams!"

Day Off

One morning, the Samurai Rangers were surprised to find that Mentor Ji had given them the day off. Emily said that she had never been on a rollercoaster before, so they decided to go to Rainbow's End, a fantastic amusement park. Jayden said he would stay behind.

"There's something I need to do," he told the others mysteriously.

When they arrived at the amusement park, Mia, Mike and Emily were raring to go, but Kevin was feeling uneasy and wanted to return to the Shiba House.

"Maybe this is a test," he told the others. "I thought a Samurai never took a day off."

But the others persuaded him to stay and join in the fun, if only for a little while.

Back at the Shiba House, Jayden was trying out the Beetle Disc, a secret and powerful disc. He knew that he had to double his power to be able to master it, but he was determined to try it out. Carefully taking the Beetle Disc from its case, Jayden put it onto his Spin Sword and prepared for action, but the disc was too powerful for him to use and he was thrown backwards, landing heavily on the ground.

"You're not ready to use the Beetle Disc yet," said Mentor Ji, who had come outside to see what was happening.

Mentor Ji explained to Jayden that a Samurai Ranger needed to give 100 per cent both mentally and physically, and that by pushing himself too hard, he wouldn't be at his best.

"Maybe I am pushing myself too hard," said Jayden, "but I'm the Red Ranger now – I have to be the best and keep getting better."

"We've always trained hard, but we used to find time for fun, too," replied Mentor Ji. "I know you wanted to go to the amusement park with the others."

However, Jayden insisted that he wanted to continue training with the powerful Beetle Disc.

"The Nighlok grow stronger by the day," he said firmly. "I must master this Beetle Disc before it's too late."

Meanwhile, the other Rangers were ready for some fun on the rides at the amusement park. All of a sudden, a Nighlok squirmed through a gap into our world. It was Dreadhead, a very powerful Nighlok. Mike, Kevin, Mia and Emily quickly morphed into Power Rangers. As the crowds in the amusement park ran away screaming, the Rangers began to fight Dreadhead, but their swords didn't seem to hurt him at all and they were thrown to the ground by the monster's mighty force.

Just as Dreadhead was about to finish them off, the Red Ranger appeared. The Red Ranger fought bravely, but even he was unable to harm the monster – his sword just went right through him.

"Our weapons don't work on this Nighlok," said the Red Ranger. "Let's all use our swords together."

The Rangers each attached their Power Discs to their Spin Swords and unleashed the full force of their special powers, but even that did little more than tickle the Nighlok.

The Red Ranger pulled the Beetle Disc from his buckle.

   "Wow! I haven't seen that before, what is it?" asked the Pink Ranger.

   But before the Red Ranger could answer her, Dreadhead began drying out. He'd been away from the Sanzu River for too long and needed to return to the Netherworld.

   "Next time you won't be so lucky! Later, Rangers!" he called as he slunk back into the Netherworld.

火 火 火

Back at the Shiba House, the Rangers were worried that their weapons hadn't worked on Dreadhead.

"Just think what might have happened to us if he hadn't dried out," said Kevin.

"No thanks," said Emily. "I'd rather think of a way to defeat him."

"Exactly," said Mentor Ji. "Fear is the enemy. If you believe in yourselves, you can win any battle."

Jayden showed the other Rangers the Beetle Disc, explaining that it was one of the secret Power Discs passed down by previous generations of Samurai. Most of the secret discs had been lost in battle, and the Beetle Disc may be the only one left.

"I'm trying to master its power," said Jayden.

"So that's why you stayed behind today," said Mike.

Jayden was determined to master the Beetle Disc.

Back in the Netherworld, Master Xandred was pleased with Dreadhead, but Dayu teased him.

"You're pathetic," she told him. "If you hadn't dried out when you did, you could have destroyed those Rangers."

Master Xandred told Dayu there was no hurry. Dreadhead could soak in the waters of the Sanzu and rest a while. When he went back to finish off the Rangers, they would be totally defenceless.

It wasn't long before Dreadhead returned for the second round, but the Samurai Rangers were waiting for him. The Red Ranger was exhausted from training all night, but he was determined to focus his power and beat Dreadhead. Using the secret Beetle Disc, he prepared for action.

"Fire Smasher, Cannon Blast Mode!" he shouted, and his sword threw out a massive blast of fire that sent Dreadhead flying.

"Rangers!" yelled the Red Ranger, "lend me your Power Discs."

The other four Rangers gave him their discs. The Red Ranger loaded all five Power Discs onto his Fire Smasher. At last, he had mastered the Beetle Disc and now his Fire Smasher could become a Five Disc Beetle Cannon. If that didn't destroy Dreadhead, then nothing could!

The Red Ranger unleashed the power of all five Power Discs at Dreadhead, defeating the Nighlok. But the biggest battle of all was only just beginning. When a Nighlok is destroyed, it comes right back as a MegaMonster. The Samurai Rangers activated MegaMode ready for battle.

"MegaMode Power! Zords Combine!" cried all five Rangers.

The five Zords combined to form the Megazord, but even with the enormous Katana at the Megazord's side, their power was not enough to defeat Dreadhead.

"You're cruising to a losing!" said Dreadhead, taunting the Rangers.

"It's time to unleash the true power of this disc," said the Red Ranger as he walked bravely out onto the Megazord's shoulder, then hurled the Beetle Disc into the air.

"BeetleZord!" he called as the Beetle Disc morphed into a BeetleZord. The other Rangers were amazed.

"A BeetleZord came out of that disc – how cool!" exclaimed the Pink Ranger.

"Time to load up," said the Red Ranger as he jumped into the cockpit of the BeetleZord. "Let's put this thing in drive and get to it!"

When the BeetleZord attacked Dreadhead and knocked him over, the MegaMonster knew he was in trouble and called for help from his Moogers. The battle had begun.

"Samurai Artillery!" shouted the Red Ranger as the BeetleZord split apart and attached itself to the Megazord, combining to become the Beetle Blaster Megazord.

Back in the Megazord cockpit, the Red Ranger fired the Beetle Cannon at the Moogers.

"Now it's your turn," said the Red Ranger to Dreadhead, who was no match for the rotating Beetle Blaster. Dreadhead was finally destroyed!

The next day, the Rangers went back to the amusement park – and this time Jayden went with them. The Samurai Rangers finally had a day off together!

I've Got a Spell on Blue

Kevin, the Blue Ranger, was practising his sword skills with Jayden, the Red Ranger, one morning at the Shiba House.

"Wow! Kevin's technique is really good," said Mia.

"They're both so good, I hate to think what would happen if they had to fight each other," added Mike.

"That would NEVER happen," said Emily.

Meanwhile, deep down in the Netherworld, Deker was talking to Master Xandred.

"I want to go after the Red Ranger, the leader of the Samurai Rangers," said Deker.

"Do what you will," snarled Master Xandred. "My head is pounding. I can only deal with one headache at a time."

Deker knew that his master was still suffering from when the last Red Ranger had sealed him down in the Netherworld. It would be some time before he fully recovered his strength. With Master Xandred's permission, Deker left to continue his quest.

Just as Deker was leaving, a Nighlok named Madimot came aboard Master Xandred's ship, boasting that he was in control of the Red Ranger's long-lost TigerZord. When the earth had cracked open and the last Red Ranger had sealed Master Xandred in the Netherworld, the TigerZord fell in the crevice, too. Madimot saved it and used his mind-control powers to make the Zord his pet. Now he planned to turn the TigerZord against the Rangers.

As Madimot entered our world, the Gap Sensor at the Shiba House lit up to alert the Samurai Rangers.

In a flash, the Rangers were ready to confront him, but were amazed to see that he had the powerful TigerZord under his power.

The Rangers knew they must get the TigerZord back, but Madimot shot out a mind-controlling ray at the Rangers.

"Everyone duck!" yelled the Red Ranger.

But the Green Ranger was too slow and the ray was coming right at him. Bravely, the Blue Ranger pushed the Green Ranger out of the way and the ray hit him instead. The Blue Ranger was now under Madimot's evil control and started to fight his fellow Rangers. Madimot sent a mind-control blast towards the Red Ranger, who countered the ray with his special Resist Disc.

水 水 水 水

Although the Rangers fought well, Madimot had both the Blue Ranger and the TigerZord on his side, and managed to overpower the Green, Yellow and Pink Rangers. The Red Ranger had no choice but to use his powers to transport the others to safety, leaving the Blue Ranger and the TigerZord with Madimot. But Madimot was drying out and needed to get back to the Sanzu River for a soak that would recharge his power.

"You wait here until I get back," he said as he ordered the Blue Ranger to stay with the TigerZord.

While Madimot was busy in the Netherworld, Deker was in our world. Being only half Nighlok, he was not so interested in harming humans – instead his wish was to fight the ultimate duel. Fighting the Red Ranger would fulfil that desire, and Deker needed to keep tabs on his future opponent, for one day they would meet in battle.

Meanwhile, Madimot couldn't resist having some fun with the Blue Ranger, who was still in his power. Together, they were causing mayhem at a local construction site. Not wanting to endanger his fellow Rangers, Jayden set off to face Madimot and the Blue Ranger alone. When Mia, Mike and Emily realized this, they followed him, knowing that it was their duty to help.

Meanwhile, Jayden was facing an impossible choice – if he didn't fight the Blue Ranger, Madimot would order the Blue Ranger to turn his sword on himself. Shortly after the other Rangers arrived, Jayden morphed into the Red Ranger and began his unwilling battle with the Blue Ranger.

As the Rangers watched the fight, they were unaware that a nearby stranger was Deker in human form. After watching the Red Ranger fight, Deker was more certain than ever that the Red Ranger was the right opponent for the ultimate duel.

As the Red Ranger fought, he tried to get close enough to the Blue Ranger to use the Resist Disc to break Madimot's spell. Attaching it to his Spin Sword, he freed him from the Nighlok's control.

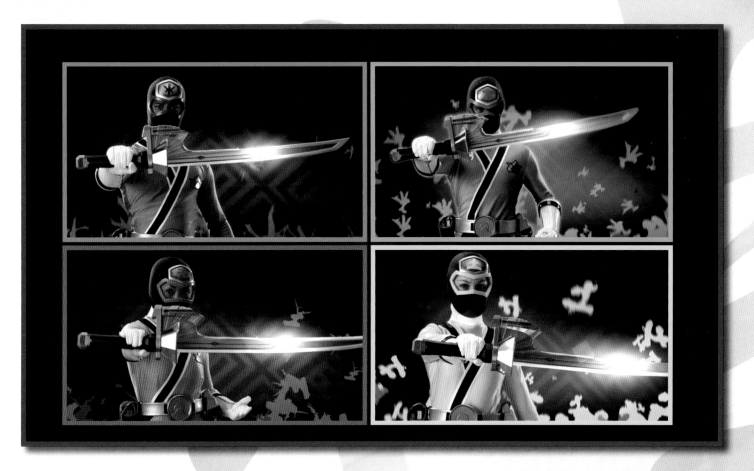

Now that all the Rangers were a team again, they morphed and sprang into action to help battle Madimot.

"You guys take care of the Nighlok. I'll handle the TigerZord," said the Red Ranger.

While the others raced off to battle Madimot, the Red Ranger prepared to face the TigerZord.

"LionZord! MegaMode Power!" he yelled as he wrote the magic Kanji Symbol that would summon his Zord.

As soon as he was in the cockpit, the TigerZord charged at the LionZord with its claws spinning. This was tougher than the Red Ranger had thought, but as soon as he was able to knock down the TigerZord, the Red Ranger leaped into the Zord and placed the Resist Disc in the control panel.

"TigerZord! Resist Power!" he yelled, and Madimot's power was lifted once again.

The TigerZord was back where it belonged.

With the whole team against him, Madimot was soon defeated – but every Nighlok has a second life as a MegaMonster!

The Red Ranger and the TigerZord began battling Madimot while the other Rangers went into MegaMode, ready to help him.

After they all morphed into MegaMode, the Red Ranger wrote the magic Kanji Symbol for 'combination' and the five Zords combined to form the massive Megazord.

"Samurai Megazord! We are united!" shouted the Rangers together.

"Samurai Artillery!" yelled the Red Ranger, and the TigerZord combined with the Megazord.

"Tiger Drill Megazord! Armed for battle!" shouted all the Rangers together in the Megazord cockpit.

The Tiger Drill Megazord and Madimot battled fiercely. Even Madimot's powerful shield was no match for the Tiger Drill, and before long Madimot was defeated for good.

"Samurai Rangers, victory is ours!" said the Red Ranger triumphantly.

Another battle against a Nighlok had been won, but the Red Ranger knew there would be more to come. A Samurai Ranger is always on guard!

Jayden, the Red Ranger, is the only Ranger with the power to seal Master Xandred and the Nighlok back in the Netherworld. Master Xandred and the Nighlok monsters were getting stronger by the day.

The Samurai Rangers would have lost their last battle with Robtish if it hadn't been for the half-human Nighlok, Deker, stepping in to save the Red Ranger. He wanted to save the Red Ranger for himself, believing it was his destiny to battle Jayden in the ultimate duel. The Samurai Rangers had been wounded in their last battle and Jayden didn't want to put them in any more danger. He felt he must defeat the Nighlok alone.

When Master Xandred discovered how Deker had saved the Red Ranger, he was furious and went with his Moogers to destroy Deker. But Deker, who was more powerful than Master Xandred had realized, managed to get away.

"This is far from over!" roared Master Xandred as Deker made his escape.

Robtish was still angry with Deker, too. He decided to squirm his way through a gap back into our world to have another go at defeating the Red Ranger.

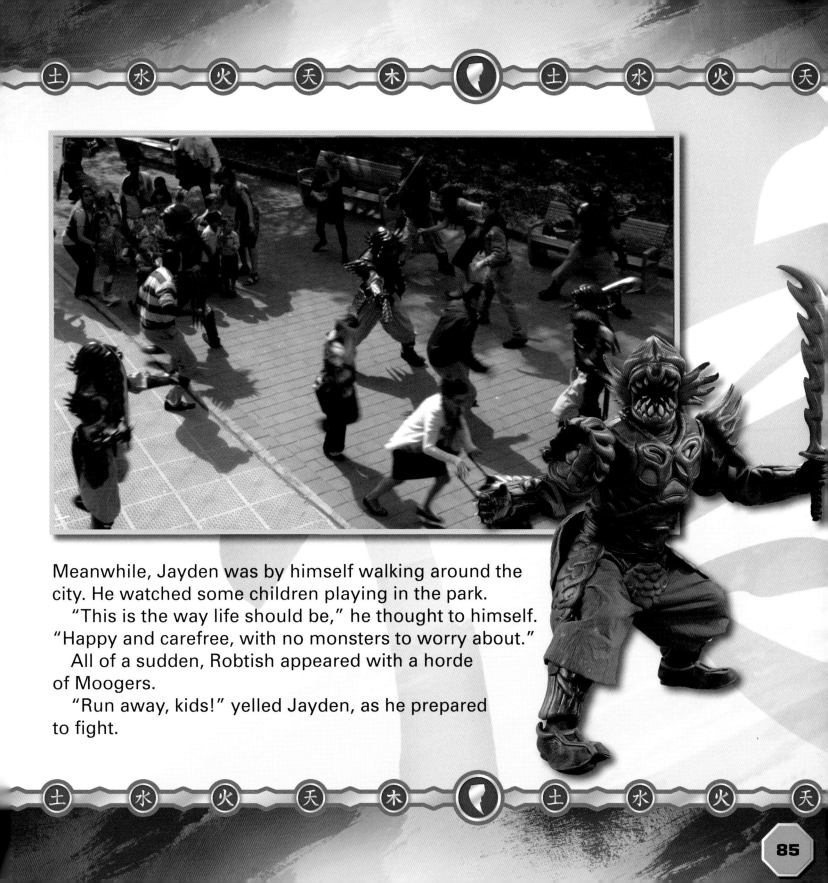

Meanwhile, Jayden was by himself walking around the city. He watched some children playing in the park.

"This is the way life should be," he thought to himself. "Happy and carefree, with no monsters to worry about."

All of a sudden, Robtish appeared with a horde of Moogers.

"Run away, kids!" yelled Jayden, as he prepared to fight.

Back at the Shiba House, the other Rangers were worried about Jayden.

"Jayden doesn't want to put you in any more danger," explained Mentor Ji to the other Rangers. "This is something he wants to do alone."

However, when the Gap Sensor went off, they wanted to go and help Jayden.

"We're in this together," said Mia. "We can't let Jayden do this by himself." The other Rangers agreed and, together, they raced off to help.

When they arrived on the scene, the Rangers told Jayden they were in this together.

"Somebody's got to stop the Nighlok," Jayden told his friends, "and I'm glad it's us!"

"Rangers together! Samurai forever!" chanted the team as they morphed into Samurai Rangers, ready to fight.

Working as a team, the Rangers soon defeated the Moogers before facing off against Robtish.

Now the battle was between Robtish and the Samurai Rangers. Using his Samurai senses, the Red Ranger was able to predict Robtish's next move. He warned the Rangers to be ready for Robtish to send out a shock wave. While the Rangers deflected the wave, Jayden was getting ready with a trick of his own.

"Say hello to my Fire Smasher!" the Red Ranger shouted.

"Five Disc Tiger Cannon – Rangers, lend me your discs!" he called to the others.

With their combined powers, the Samurai Rangers overcame Robtish. However, within seconds, Robtish came back to fight some more, this time as a MegaMonster.

"Lion FoldingZord! Turtle FoldingZord! Dragon FoldingZord! Bear FoldingZord! Ape FoldingZord!" cried out each of the Rangers in turn.

"MegaMode Power!" they all shouted together.

In MegaMode, the Rangers were very powerful, but they were never stronger than when they worked as a team.

"Zords, combine!" they commanded in unison.

The five Zords locked together to form the awesome Megazord. Now the Samurai Rangers felt ready for anything. But they were shocked about the MegaMonster's next trick – flying Moogers!

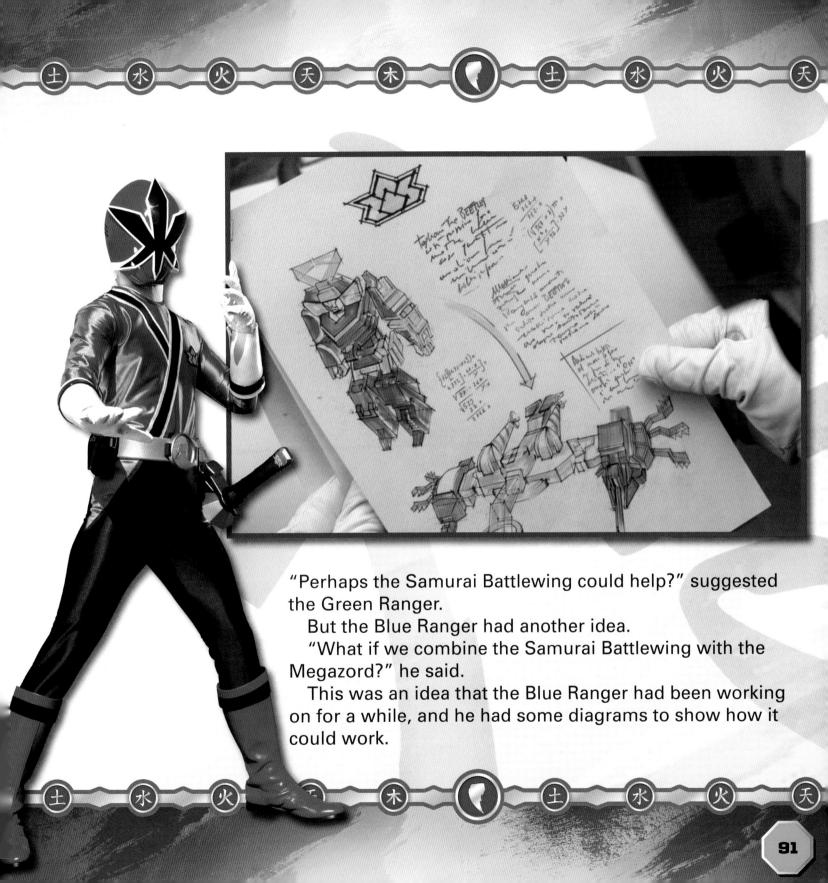

"Perhaps the Samurai Battlewing could help?" suggested the Green Ranger.

But the Blue Ranger had another idea.

"What if we combine the Samurai Battlewing with the Megazord?" he said.

This was an idea that the Blue Ranger had been working on for a while, and he had some diagrams to show how it could work.

"First, we must combine the TigerZord, the BeetleZord and the SwordfishZord to create the Samurai Battlewing," said the Blue Ranger as he sprang into action.

The Samurai Battlewing blasted one shot at Robtish to distract him while it split into pieces and attached itself to the Megazord.

It was now a Battlewing Megazord that Robtish and his flying Moogers had to face.

Now that the Megazord could fly, it wasn't long before the flying Moogers were wiped out.

"Bye, bye, birdies!" laughed the Yellow Ranger.

It was just Robtish that the Rangers had to battle.

"Looks like we saved the worst for last," said the Red Ranger, as they prepared to fight.

Robtish was very powerful, but the Rangers launched an aerial attack on him.

"Let's fly up so we can take him down," said the Blue Ranger.

The Samurai Rangers activated their Mega Blades, and from way up in the air they dived down on the MegaMonster. With one great slash of their mighty blade, Robtish was finally defeated.

水 水 水

"Samurai Rangers, victory is ours!" said the Red Ranger proudly.

The Red Ranger knew there was still a lot of work left to do before the Nighlok were defeated, but he was very glad he had his team there to help him do it.

Unexpected Arrival

A young man on a mission was making his way into town one morning. Where he was heading was a mystery, but one that would soon be revealed.

At the Shiba House, the Gap Sensor was flashing. The Rangers hurried off, ready to fight whatever evil awaited them. However, when they got to where the Sensor had been set off, there wasn't a Nighlok in sight.

"Perhaps the Gap Sensor isn't working," suggested Kevin.

But when they checked it, they found it was working fine. The Rangers went back to the Shiba House, feeling puzzled. But Jayden felt sure he could sense a presence, even though none of the other Rangers could.

Deep down in the dark Netherworld, a Nighlok named Vulpes was up to no good. With his special inter-dimensional mirror, he had been spying on Jayden to try and find out his secret Sealing Symbol – the magic symbol that he would use one day to seal Master Xandred and the Nighlok monsters back in the Netherworld for good.

Back at the Shiba House, there was a loud swishing sound, followed by a thud as something hit the wall of the Shiba House. The Rangers rushed outside to see what it was. They found an arrow stuck in the wall with a message written in black ink attached. It said SEE YOU SOON! None of the Rangers knew what this meant or who could have sent it, although Mike noticed that the message smelled of fish.

Jayden was still sure that something had invaded their house, even though it was protected from the Nighlok by magic Power Symbols.

"Are you sure you're not imagining things?" asked Mia.

But Mentor Ji had always taught Jayden to trust his instincts, so that was what he intended to do. He felt as if somebody was watching him all the time and he knew things weren't right. The only time the feeling stopped was when he was near water. This gave Jayden an idea.

Later that day, Mike, Mia, Emily and Kevin went out to check the area where the Gap Sensor had gone off. They were still worried that something might be wrong. While they were out, they noticed a young man selling fish. He was handing out leaflets, and Emily noticed that the writing on them matched the writing on the mysterious note. When they questioned the young man, he was shocked. He realized who he was talking with.

"No, you're going to ruin my big moment," he said as he ran away.

Just then, Mike got a call from Mentor Ji. He told them that Jayden had gone to Spring Valley on his own. Kevin and Mia decided to follow Jayden, leaving Mike and Emily to chase after the mysterious fish seller.

Down in the Netherworld, Vulpes was watching Jayden through his magic mirror. Jayden was standing by a lake and practising his Sealing Symbol. Vulpes felt sure he would soon learn the secret of the magic Sealing Symbol. However, as he watched, smoke filled the mirror, clouding Vulpes' view. When the smoke cleared, Jayden was nowhere to be seen. Vulpes was furious and decided to challenge Jayden face to face.

Meanwhile, Emily and Mike were still chasing the fish man, who was really giving them the runaround. They stopped to catch their breath, but couldn't see the mysterious man anywhere.

When Vulpes arrived at Spring Valley the Red Ranger sprang at the Nighlok from out of the sacred Spring Valley waters. Vulpes didn't see him coming, and the Red Ranger grabbed the magic mirror from Vulpes.

The Red Ranger chose this place to face the Nighlok because the water in our world is more pure than that in the Sanzu River and it blocked Vulpes' view.

Just then, the Blue and Pink Rangers turned up to help. When they saw Vulpes, the Pink Ranger called Mike and Emily.

"Come on," Mike told Emily after taking the call, "the others need our help to fight a Nighlok over in Spring Valley."

What Mike and Emily didn't know was that the fish man was hiding behind a post and listening to every word.

"This sounds like a perfect time for my big moment," he said to himself when Mike and Emily had left.

Back at Spring Valley, the fight was in full swing.

"Where are the others?" asked the Red Ranger.

"They were chasing the fish man, but they're on their way now," replied Kevin.

"Huh?" said Jayden, who didn't have any idea what Kevin was talking about.

"Try this spell, Fox Fire!" Vulpes yelled as he threw out a stream of fire at the Red Ranger, knocking him off his feet.

Luckily, the other Rangers arrived to help. They combined the force of their weapons, but Vulpes used his Fox Reflection Spell to turn the power of the Rangers' weapons back against them, and they were all flung to the ground.

天木火水土

Out of nowhere, a shower of Barracuda Bombs flew at Vulpes, knocking him over. It was the fish man!

"Now, this is a big moment. Man, this is going to be so golden," he announced.

The Rangers couldn't believe their eyes when the stranger pulled a gadget from his pocket.

"Samurai Morpher! Gold Power!" he shouted, and the Rangers were amazed to see the young man morph into a Gold Samurai Ranger.

"Gold is good to go!" he said as he stood before Vulpes.

The Samurai Rangers were stunned. They had never heard of a Gold Ranger before!
The Gold Ranger readied himself to face Vulpes, but the Nighlok called upon a horde
of Moogers to battle for him. Moving faster than the eye could see, the Gold Ranger
dispatched the Moogers with the legendary Sheath Slash manoeuvre.

As the Gold Ranger continued to battle Vulpes by himself, the Red Ranger dived in to help. Combining their forces, they soon defeated Vulpes. When Vulpes came back moments later as a MegaMonster, the Rangers knew that it would take all five of them to wipe him out. Going into MegaMode, the Rangers combined to become the Battlewing Megazord and prepared to fight. But Vulpes still had some tricks up his sleeve.

"Fox Veil!" he cried, wrapping himself in a veil of invisibility.

"How can we fight him if we can't see him?" asked the Pink Ranger.

Just then, the Gold Ranger activated his own MegaMode and the Rangers were amazed to see that he had his own Zord – the OctoZord.

"Could this guy really be a genuine Ranger after all?" asked the Pink Ranger.

The OctoZord sprayed a cloud of inky mist and Vulpes was revealed. Then the OctoZord's tentacles knocked the MegaMonster off its feet. Now the Battlewing Megazord had a chance to strike with their Megazord's Katana Blade! Vulpes fell to the ground, defeated at last.

"Samurai Rangers, victory is ours!" said Jayden.

After the battle, when the Gold Ranger demorphed, Jayden recognized him at once as his childhood friend, Antonio. Many years ago, Jayden had given Antonio his OctoZord as a parting gift. Antonio had vowed that they would meet again, both as Samurai Rangers. All the Rangers agreed that Antonio had definitely delivered his golden moment!

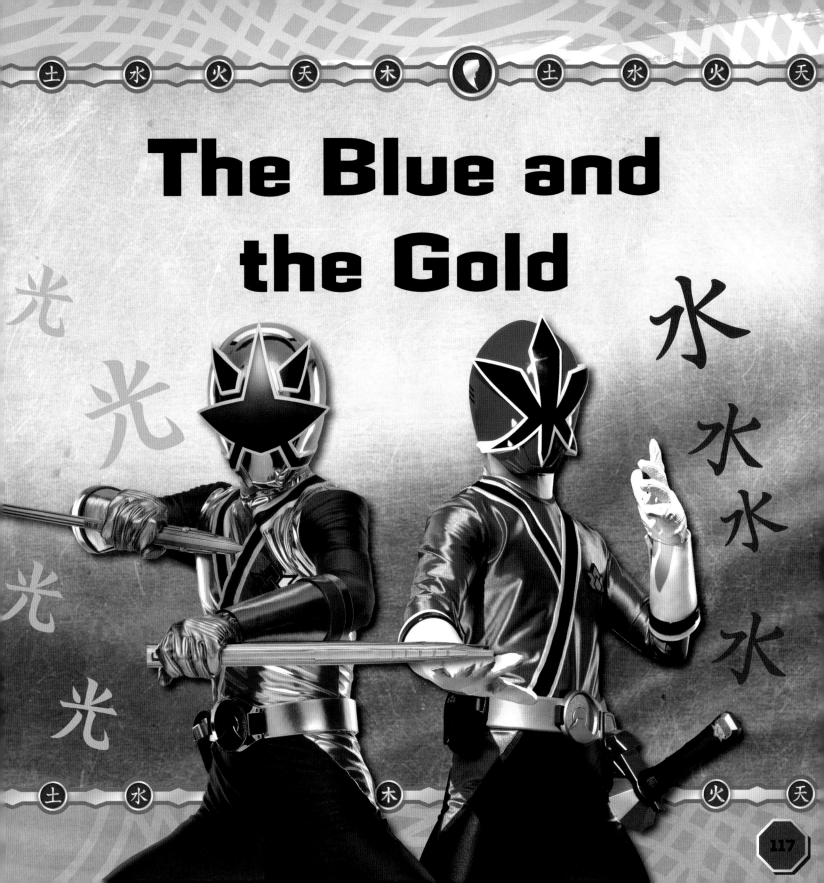

The Blue and the Gold

At the Shiba House, Antonio, the Gold Ranger, was showing the other Rangers the ClawZord. Mentor Ji had hidden away the battle-damaged Zord for years.

"Mentor asked me to perform a bit of my tech-whizz magic," said Antonio, pleased to have this important responsibility.

As the Rangers stared at him, fascinated by the new Zord, Antonio reached for his Samuraizer and pressed a button to make Samurai symbols appear.

Antonio thought that showing the Rangers his hi-tech skills could help prove him to be a worthy Samurai Ranger. However, Kevin thought differently – Antonio was showing he was a computer nerd, not a Samurai.

"I know I wasn't born into the Samurai life like you guys, but I'm trying to help in my own way," Antonio said, realizing how difficult it would be to convince Kevin.

Later, Mike, Mia and Emily spoke to Antonio, and Antonio explained that he felt he had already proved himself in battle.

"Eat, drink, sleep being a Samurai. It's the only way to impress him," said Mike, knowingly.

From now on, Antonio knew it was his mission to prove himself to Kevin.

Down in the dark Netherworld, Dayu was telling Master Xandred that Octoroo was working on a big scheme, and if it worked, all Nighlok would be able to escape the Sanzu River for good.

"Huh! Good!" snarled Master Xandred. "If that squid brain can really pull it off, then putting up with that lame blabbermouth all these years will be worth it!"

Back in our world, Octoroo was looking down a dark well, deep inside a forest.

"Kiddies' eyes will be crying and Nighlok will have a place to get wet when they're drying!" Octoroo cackled.

The Nighlok Antberry then set out to steal children's toys, followed by a horde of Moogers.

At the Shiba House, Antonio was working on his plan to prove himself to Kevin. He planted tiny cameras around the house in order to spy on Kevin's every move. At the stroke of midnight, when Kevin finally tucked himself into bed, Antonio went to bed, too.

Meanwhile, the Nighlok Antberry was using his sneaky skills to steal every child's toy in sight. Antberry targeted Bulk and Spike, stealing Spike's favourite teddy bear mascot. The next morning, Bulk and Spike could see a trail of slime where the teddy bear once sat!

At the Shiba House the next day, Antonio was spying on Kevin as he prepared to go for a run.

"Training and more training. Everything precisely timed," Antonio said quietly to himself.

Antonio decided to follow him into the forest. Suddenly, an evil chuckle rang out through the trees, stopping Kevin in his tracks.

"Did you hear that, Antonio?" asked Kevin, a little way ahead of Antonio.

Antonio couldn't believe Kevin knew he'd been spying on him!

"So, why the spy cams?" Kevin asked, frustrated.

"I just wanted to see what a true Samurai does," replied Antonio.

Kevin explained that being a Samurai was the real deal – it wasn't like being in a spy movie. However, he knew that right now they had to work together to find out where the evil laugh was coming from.

Deep in the forest, Octoroo was looking at all of the toys Antberry had managed to steal from children.

"It's brilliant! By tossing exactly 30 beloved toys in the well, the sorrow it causes will make the river rise and fill the well once again!" said Octoroo, quickly instructing Antberry to get to work chopping up the toys.

Before the well dried up a while ago, it was the Nighlok's main portal into the real world. Octoroo needed to get it working once again!

Kevin and Antonio were perched behind a nearby rock, watching their every move. Reaching for his Samuraizer, Kevin tried to get hold of Jayden, but the signals were blocked. Suddenly, Octoroo struck the rock with a fiery blast, and Kevin and Antonio quickly morphed into the Blue and Gold Rangers. Octoroo had put up secret barriers, which had jammed their phone signals, so they were unable to get help.

"Time to enjoy my new toy! Sanzu slime!" shouted Antberry, as he blasted a sheet of slime over the Rangers.

"Hey! My blade's as slippery as an eel!" cried the Gold Ranger, unable to keep hold of his Barracuda Blade.

The Blue and Gold Rangers left their weapons behind and started to fight Antberry with their Samurai moves. But Antberry was too slippery for them to get a grip on!

Octoroo joined in by blasting them into the air. Then he unleashed the Moogers on them.

"Alright, Moogers, go finish those pests off!" Octoroo ordered.

Back at the Shiba House, the others were wondering where Kevin and Antonio were.

"I've got a bad feeling about this," Jayden told the others.

In the forest, Kevin still couldn't get a signal on his phone. With Antonio's arm now injured, he decided to fight the Nighlok alone. However, within minutes, Kevin was cornered by Moogers.

"Back off, Moogers!" shouted Antonio, coming to Kevin's rescue.

Antonio managed to take down the Moogers, but Kevin was annoyed that he had stepped in and put himself at risk.

"Being a Samurai is more than just following ancient traditions," Antonio said. "It's about being a warrior, a protector of all things good."

Kevin realized Antonio was right, and he had the true spirit of a Samurai. He told Antonio the other Rangers would turn up soon, as he wasn't at the house in time for practice.

As Kevin and Antonio reached the top of a slope, a wall of Moogers stood waiting.

"Take a deep breath, 'cause the battle's about to begin," said Antonio.

They quickly morphed into the Blue and Gold Rangers and went head-to-head with the Moogers, defeating the Moogers in seconds. Just as Antberry was about to chop up the first toy, the Rangers attacked, and the evil axe fell into the well.

"Even if you can hold your weapons, you can't slip away from me!" cried Antberry, knocking both Rangers to the ground.

Suddenly, a huge fire-strike sent Octoroo and Antberry flying. The other Samurai Rangers had come to the rescue!

The Red Ranger's blazing strike overpowered Antberry's sheet of slime, and quickly turned him into a fiery blaze. The Rangers' amazing Samurai moves then finished him off, sending him into the dark well.

Within moments, Antberry turned into a MegaMonster, ready to fight!

"MegaMode Power!" the Rangers shouted in unison.

The Rangers jumped into their Zord cockpits, joined by the Gold Ranger with his special OctoZord.

"Octo Spear Megazord! Armed for battle!" the Rangers cried.

The Megazord wasn't able to get a grip on the slimy Antberry, so they blasted out ice to freeze him. Then they used their electric spear to take him down for good!

When they returned to the Shiba House, all they had left to do was give back the stolen toys to the children.

"We get to make things right. That's the great thing about being a Samurai, right Antonio?" said Kevin.

Antonio had proven himself to be a great Ranger in battle and Kevin had finally accepted him into their Samurai team.

Team Spirit

One morning at the Shiba House, Mia, Mike, Kevin and Jayden were hiding from Emily, as they were preparing food and decorations for her secret birthday party the next day. As soon as Mia offered to bake a birthday cake, the others quickly explained that Antonio had ordered one already – her baking was that bad!

In the depths of the Netherworld, Octoroo noticed something was wrong with Master Xandred.

"He's like a stick of dynamite with a really short fuse! We need to be careful not to upset the big guy," Octoroo warned Dayu.

Meanwhile, Antonio was sitting on a riverbank, eager to catch a nice big fish for Emily's birthday. In a box behind him sat his injured ClawZord.

"She was so cool!" said Antonio about Emily, to his ClawZord. "And she accepted me right into the group from the start."

Then Antonio promised to have the ClawZord up and running again in no time.

In the Netherworld, Octoroo could see the Nighlok getting stronger and stronger as the Sanzu River continued to rise. Suddenly, the menacing Splitface climbed onto the boat .

"And I'll go scare those human crybabies to raise it even higher!" said Splitface to Dayu and Octoroo.

Meanwhile, Deker was in our world.

"Master Xandred's binds can't hold me," Deker said to himself. "But my cursed half-human, half-Nighlok existence still imprisons me. My fate is sealed."

As Deker walked, Antonio was walking towards him, pulling his fishing cart. Unaware of Deker's true identity, Antonio invited Deker to have a fish lunch with him. But Deker was on a mission, so he declined and walked away. Suddenly, Jayden called Antonio to alert him of a Nighlok attack.

In the city, the scary Splitface was already creating havoc. He was stealing people's spirits, causing them to fall into a deep sleep.

"I have such a sweet tooth for spirited snacks!" Splitface announced.

Just then, Splitface was targeted by a burst of electricity that immediately knocked him to the ground. The Samurai Rangers leaped into action against the Nighlok, but found Splitface impossible to fight once his body separated into lots of evil faces, which flew around them in a swarm.

Suddenly, Splitface cornered Emily, stealing her spirit and sending her into a deep sleep. Splitface then told the Rangers his evil plan.

"Her spirit was delicious! And in 24 hours, it will be mine forever," said Splitface.

Only if the Rangers defeated him would they be able to reclaim the stolen spirits. However, Splitface was heading back to the Netherworld where humans couldn't follow. And he wasn't planning on coming back! The Rangers had to think of something – they couldn't lose Emily forever!

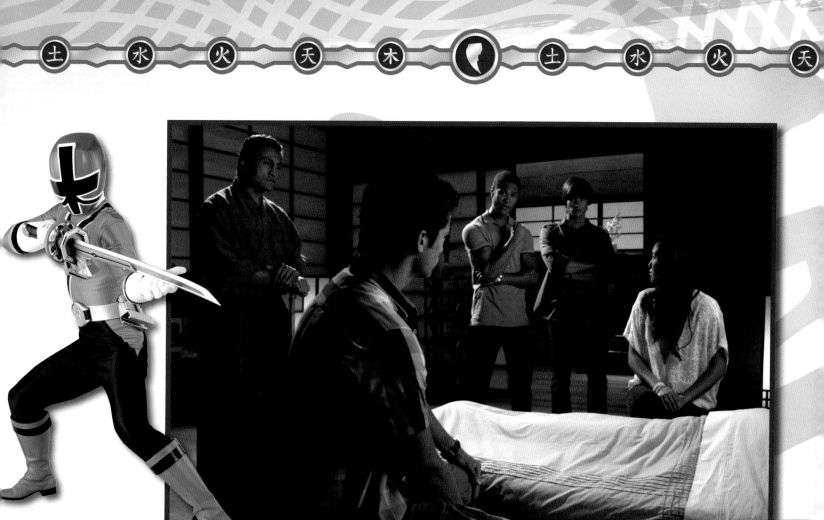

At the Shiba House, the Rangers sat beside Emily as she lay fast asleep. Mentor Ji told them that Splitface had stolen the spirits of many other people.

"I can't believe by tomorrow night, Emily and all those people could stay asleep forever. We have to defeat that Nighlok before that happens," said Kevin worriedly.

"No matter what it takes, we have to save her," agreed Mike.

Meanwhile, Antonio had gone back to the park. He was determined to find a way to help Emily. Tapping the keys on his Samuraizer, he conjured his gold electronic Samurai symbol and threw it toward his ClawZord.

"Samurai symbol, live!" he shouted.

Antonio knew he had to get his ClawZord working again. To his dismay, the power of his electronic symbol failed to revive the damaged ClawZord.

Back at the Shiba House, Emily suddenly woke up.

"Thanks for putting on a brave face for me, but I know I'm not okay," Emily said quietly to her friends.

Within seconds, Emily was asleep again. Mike became angry and stormed out of the house, back to where they had faced Splitface earlier. Mike looked at the crack in the wall where Splitface had disappeared back to the Netherworld.

"You can't do this to Emily! Do you hear me?" screamed Mike, lashing out with his Spin Sword.

As soon as Jayden arrived, Deker suddenly appeared in human form. Deker realized that it wasn't the right time to fight the ultimate duel, so instead offered them a solution.

"There is one way for humans like you to enter the Netherworld. Simply trade your human existence to become a Nighlok. Willingly give yourself over to them and pass through the gap," Deker told the Rangers.

Suddenly, Deker transformed into his Nighlok form to show them he was living proof of this working.

Just as the team was about to throw themselves through the gap into the Netherworld, Antonio showed up. He explained a way he could draw Splitface back into the real world, using symbol power and his special ClawZord.

光

光 光 光

The Rangers lined up with their Spin Swords and hurled their symbol power at the ClawZord several times. The more power, the bigger the chance they had of finally activating the ClawZord. Suddenly, Splitface was transported from the Netherworld and appeared in front of them. It had worked!

The ClawZord threw a shocked Splitface against the wall and Antonio explained how he had brought him back.

"When we came in contact, I marked you with a symbol," Antonio told Splitface. "And after I finished programming the ClawZord, I just needed the other Rangers to help me activate it."

Jayden, Kevin, Mike, Antonio and Mia quickly morphed into Power Rangers to defeat Splitface once and for all. Now that Splitface was marked with power symbols, he could no longer separate the faces on his body.

The Red Ranger dealt a fiery blast with his mighty Fire Smasher. Just when they thought they had obliterated the Nighlok for good, he came back as a MegaMonster.

"Without Emily, we can't combine into a Megazord," the Pink Ranger said, worriedly.

But the Gold Ranger wasn't worried – he just needed to team up with his ClawZord to save the day.

The Gold Ranger jumped into the cockpit of his ClawZord and confronted the MegaMonster alone.

"Time to try out these pincer claws!" shouted the Gold Ranger.

Suddenly, giant Moogers rose up from behind the MegaMonster. The Gold Ranger targeted the Moogers with his giant claw spinners.

"Now for a big trick. ClawZord transformation!" instructed the Gold Ranger.

The ClawZord then transformed into the powerful Claw BattleZord East to take a few more Moogers down.

Then the Gold Ranger transformed into the Claw BattleZord West. However, the Moogers were shooting huge arrows at the BattleZord, and the Red Ranger knew the team had to step in and help. The Red, Blue and Green Rangers entered MegaMode and called up their animal Zords.

"Samurai Battlewing, we are united!" the three Rangers shouted in unison. The mighty Battlewing destroyed the Moogers and the ClawZord. The Gold Ranger then transformed into the strong Claw BattleZord South.

With the Claw BattleZord South's huge swords, the Gold Ranger fought against the MegaMonster.

"Double Katana, strike!" said the Gold Ranger, determined to save the spirits from Splitface.

But it still wasn't the end of the Nighlok. Calling on the Claw BattleZord East once again, the Gold Ranger defeated Splitface with its giant pincers.

Back at the Shiba House, Mentor Ji was sitting beside the sleeping Emily. Suddenly, a bright ball of light appeared and entered Emily's mouth, waking her immediately – her spirit had returned! In the nearby hospital, all the people were waking up, their spirits now saved.

"Samurai Rangers, victory is ours!" said the Red Ranger.

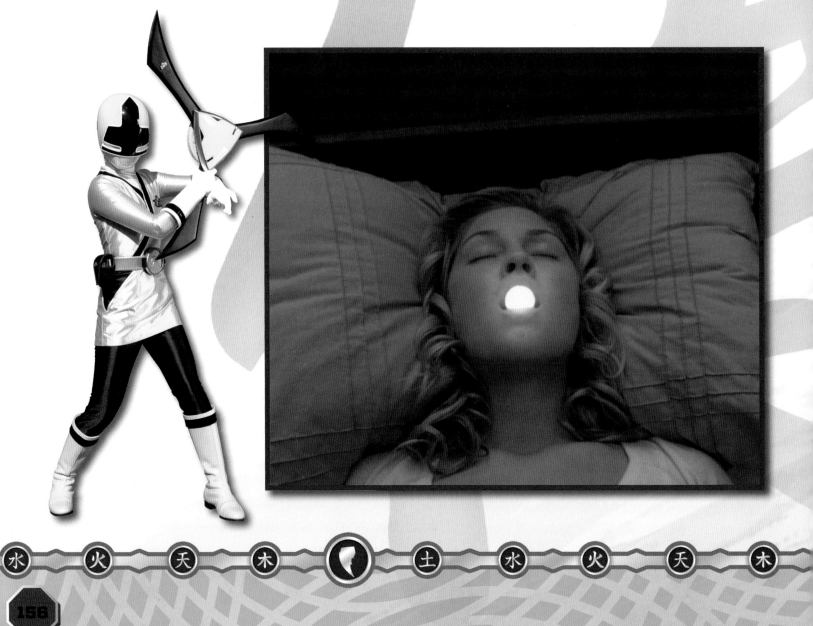

Once they all returned to the Shiba House, Mia took Emily to the others, where they were ready to give her a birthday surprise.

"You guys are the best," said Emily, as Mike presented her with a birthday card from her sister.

"No, Emily. Mike was right. You're the best. We're just so happy to see that you're okay. Today, victory really is ours!" said Jayden, happy to have his friend back.